Float
A Guide to Letting Go

by Aimee L. Ruland

Illustrated by Carl R. Anderson

Loving Healing Press

Ann Arbor, MI

Library of Congress Cataloging-in-Publication Data

Names: Ruland, Aimee L., author. | Anderson, Carl R., 1977- illustrator.
Title: Float : a guide to letting go / by Aimee L. Ruland ; illustrated by
  Carl R. Anderson.
Description: Ann Arbor, MI : Loving Healing Press, [2019] | Summary:
  Illustrations and rhyming text guide the reader in using breathwork and
  mindfulness to let go of unwanted feelings by visualizing releasing them
  into balloons of various colors, then letting them go.
Identifiers: LCCN 2019013210 (print) | LCCN 2019016933 (ebook) | ISBN
  9781615994618 (Kindle, ePub, pdf) | ISBN 9781615994595 (pbk. : alk. paper)
  | ISBN 9781615994601 (hardcover : alk. paper) | ISBN 9781615994618 (ebook)
Subjects: | CYAC: Stories in rhyme. | Emotions--Fiction. | Mindfulness
  (Psychology)--Fiction. | Breathing exercises--Fiction.
Classification: LCC PZ8.3.R882 (ebook) | LCC PZ8.3.R882 Flo 2019 (print) |
  DDC [E]--dc23
LC record available at https://lccn.loc.gov/2019013210

Published by
Loving Healing Press
5145 Pontiac Trail
Ann Arbor, MI 48105

www.LHPress.com
info@LHPress.com
Tollfree 888-761-6268
Fax 734-663-6861

Distributed by Ingram (USA/CA/AU), Bertram's Books (UK/EU)

To the sweet, gentle soul of my lovely Ava Juliette, for whom my heart beats. You are so loved.

And, to all of the many children whom I've had the honor and privilege of serving over the years. May you grow in love and light.

Let go or be dragged. -Zen Proverb

The day is done, I'm cozied in
All snug inside my bed
But, sometimes I find it tough to relax
In my heart and in my head

I know a trick that helps me
To fall asleep at night
Maybe you could try it, too
To help you—it just might

First, I relax my body
Then, I breathe deep and look inside
For anything that's keeping me
From peace in my heart and mind

I listen to my true Self
And to what my feelings have to say
About all the things that happened
During this long and busy day

If I happen to notice something
That's keeping me from rest
I imagine I'm holding a big balloon
And I take a great big breath

I breathe in a happy thought
And pull it in to my whole being
As I breathe out, I fill the balloon
And it works! It's very freeing!

It helps me to let go
Of any negative thing
Then I tie up the balloon
And let go of its long string

Come along with me
As I see what I can find
For anything I might feel
Is worth leaving far behind…

I take a moment to ask
Was someone mean to me today?
Did I feel as though I don't belong?
Or told that I can't play?

Although I might feel frustrated
Or even mad or sad
I imagine I'm holding a red balloon
And blow it up instead of feeling bad

I breathe deep and calmly
Then I tie it up mindfully
And my favorite part is letting go
As I release and set it free

Float away now, anger
Float up into the sky
Sail far away from here
I'm telling you goodbye

I know you serve a purpose
And that you're part of me
But for now, anger, I release you
I'm asking you to leave

Next, I take a moment
To think of how I interact
With everyone around me
With whom I may impact

Does my heart reflect my words?
Are my thoughts and actions kind?
Am I aware of my intentions?
Or do I turn an eye that's blind?

It's important to be me
To be strong, yet friendly, too
But I focus on what's good
And put the rest in my balloon

It's an orange balloon this time
That I'm holding in my hands
It's where I'll leave my guilt
My bossiness and demands

As I let go of these heavy things
I begin to see
It's as important for others to be them
As it is for me to be me

I feel a sudden wish
To be kind, and gentle, too
To everyone around me
To friends, both old and new

It feels good to have one another
To be connected, and to grow
Together, like the roots of trees
Planted long ago

I take a moment now
And this one can be tough--
To look at who I truly am
And remember I'm good enough

That I deserve to be loved
To be respected, and happy, too
And any time I doubt that
I know just what to do

I remember that I'm worthy
Of great and many things
That I could soar over mountains
If I trust in my own wings

I simply grab ahold
Of my bright yellow balloon
And fill it with what makes me feel empty
Like doubt and worry, too

I send it sailing over hilltops
And far beyond the clouds
Because I am no longer afraid
To be me and to be proud

Do you ever feel jealous
Of someone or something?
Maybe it's love, attention, or toys
Or even a shiny ring

That heavy feeling of longing
Can fill our hearts with greed
But, I know I can control envy
By asking it to leave

I think of all the many things
That I have, and I am grateful
Like love and trust and imagination
And, suddenly...I've got a plateful—

Of things I cherish, people I trust,
And those who love me, too
My heart feels full and overjoyed
Envy, there's no room for you

Inside of my green balloon
Is where you're meant to be
Go on now, and float away
Far upon the breeze

I have a feeling that one day
You'll be back to visit me
But, that's okay because I know
You have no control over me

I have many thoughts and feelings
Each one is special to me
But, I sometimes feel they can't be shared
In certain company

I keep things in sometimes
I bottle and I hide them
I'm afraid one day, I might just burst
If I continue to deny them

What I want is to live freely
To show my Self and speak my Truth
Without doubting things and always asking,
"Well...what's the use?"

I know what I feel matters
And I'm proud of who I am
The person who laughs and sighs and cries
And sometimes takes a stand

I fill up a blue balloon now
With anything holding me back
I stand inside my courage
And I know that I'm right on track--

To let my true Self shine
Unique, honest, and kind
And live the life I want to live
Leaving the bottles behind

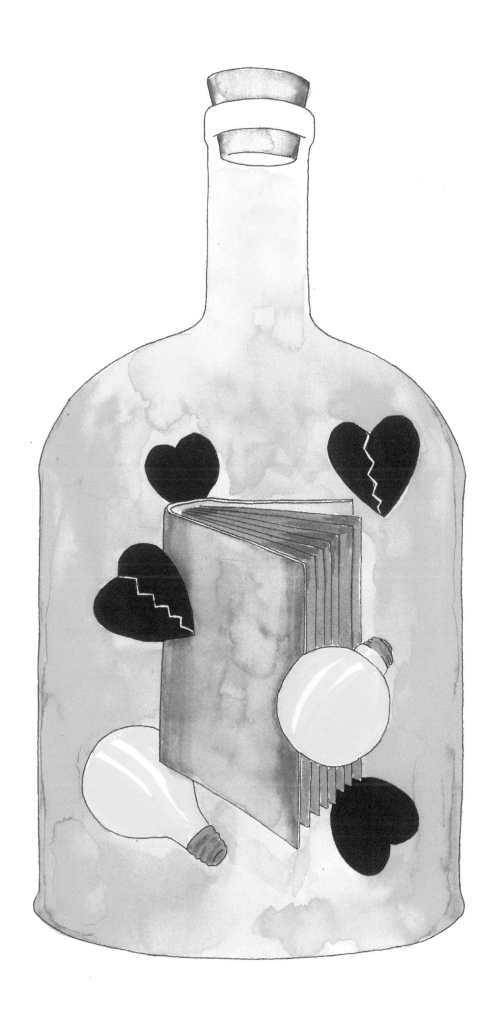

Take a moment to enjoy this release...

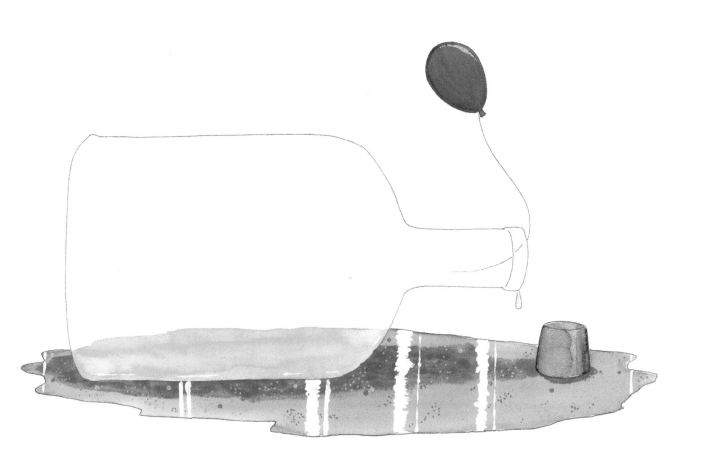

At times, I get mixed up
About what I need to do
It makes my head feel dizzy
And puts me in a mood

I get caught up in thinking
That maybe I am lost
That I don't know who to trust
Or who is really the boss

I take a breath and focus
All of this energy
Toward my indigo balloon
Then it all becomes clear to me—

If I inhale trust, and exhale fear
It really calms me down
It also helps me see that
My guiding voice wears the crown

That little voice within me
Who knows just what to do
The one who keeps me safe
And always sees me through

It's what makes me special
What really makes me, me
And it's nice to sit and listen
And enjoy the harmony

Sometimes, I feel so small
In this great big world of ours
Yet, I feel a strong connection
When I look up at the stars

Anything murky becomes clear
When I gaze at my reflection
And I feel great peace in knowing
That there's a real connection

Between you and me
The animals, the Earth, and all that I am seeing
And the great beyond—The Universe
That brought us into being

I feel so very honored
To be an important part of
An amazing place, full of amazing gifts
The greatest being love

I gently take my violet balloon
And one last deep, full breath
To release my confusion,
My feeling lost, or even selfish

I feel safe, and I feel proud
To call this place my home
And I am so incredibly grateful
To know I'm not alone

I feel so much better now
Things seem different to me, it's true
I feel light and calm and happy
And, I hope that you do, too

It's good to study our feelings
And to know which ones do serve us
In ways that help us to grow
And serve a loving purpose

It's important that we let go
Of all the many things
That could leave us feeling tangled
And caught up in their strings

There's no telling where those negative
Thoughts and feelings could swirl and roam
But, I'm certain I'd rather be here
Than out in that unknown—

Enjoying every moment
Living in the here and now
Being present, true, and mindful
With my feet upon the ground

Farewell, balloons, and thank you
For helping my view to shift
And to understand that the present
Truly is a gift

THE END!

About the author:

Aimee L. Ruland is a graduate of the University of Pittsburgh, with degree concentrations in Psychology and Philosophy. She is an Applied Metapsychology facilitator, Certified Yoga Instructor, Usui Reiki practitioner, meditation guide, and mother. She holds an affinity with birds of prey, studies in quantum mechanics, and sculpting with her daughter.

About the illustrator:

Carl R. Anderson has been an Operations Engineer for over twenty years. He enjoys carpentry, homesteading, and expressing himself artistically through a variety of media.

Aimee and Carl are husband and wife team.